Sitting In My BOX

two lions

two lions

Amazon Publishing, Attn: Amazon Children's Publishing
P.O. Box 400818, Las Vegas, NV 89140
www.amazon.com/amazonchildrenspublishing

Library of Congress Cataloging-in-Publication Data

Lillegard, Dee.
  Sitting in my box / by Dee Lillegard ; illustrated by Jon Agee.
    p. cm.
  Summary: The box in which all the animals are sitting gets more
and more crowded until a hungry flea comes along.
  ISBN 978-1-4778-4741-1
  [1. Boxes–Fiction. 2. Animals–Fiction.] I. Agee, Jon, ill. II. Title.
  PZ7.L6275Si 2010
  [E]–dc22   2009007936
Printed in China

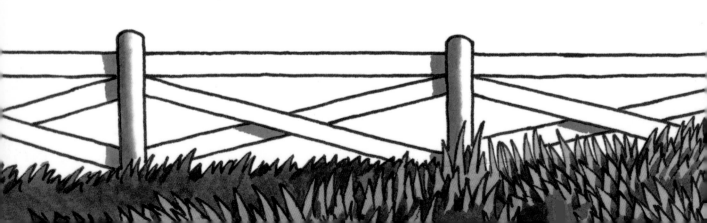

For Brett,
who remembers sitting in his box
—D.L.

Sitting In My BOX

by **Dee Lillegard**

pictures by **Jon Agee**

Sitting in my box.

A tall giraffe knocks.

"Let me, let me in."
So I move over.

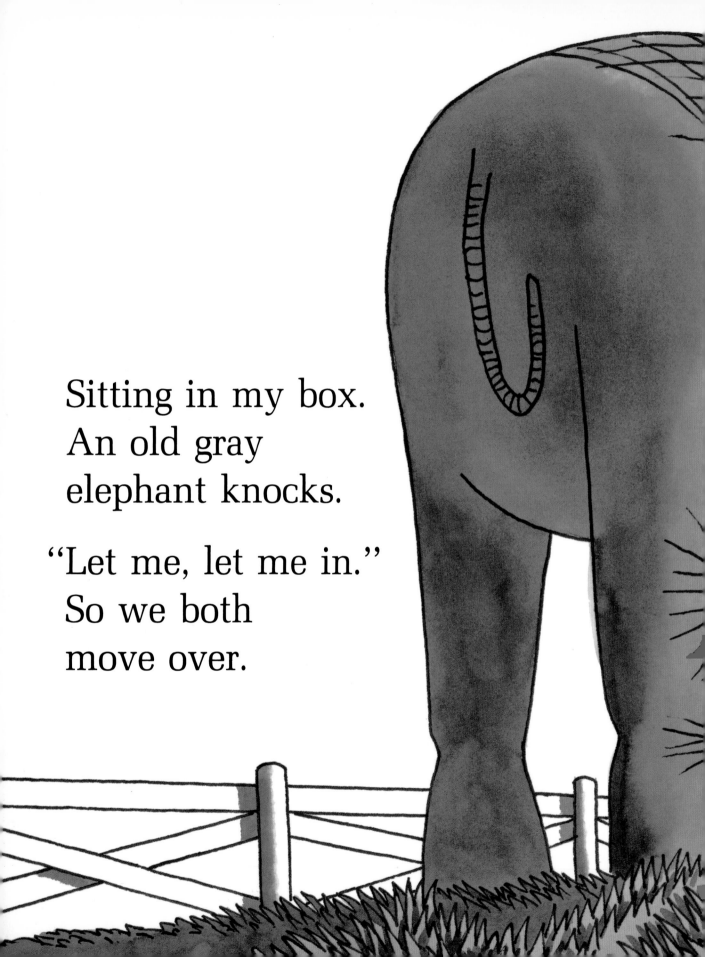

Sitting in my box.
An old gray
elephant knocks.

"Let me, let me in."
So we both
move over.

Sitting in my box.
A big baboon knocks.

"Let me, let me in."
So we all move over.

Sitting in my box.
A grumpy lion knocks.

"Let me, let me in."
So we all move over.

Sitting in my box.
A hippopotamus knocks.

"Let me, let me in."
So we *all* move over.

Standing in my box.
There's no room to sit.

"Wait a minute!
This box has
too much in it."

"Someone has to go."

"Not me."

"Not me."

"Not me."

"Not me."

"Not me."

Sitting in my box.
Along comes a flea.
A flea *never* knocks.
He jumps right in.

He bites the hippo
and the grumpy lion.

He bites the baboon
and the old gray
elephant.

He bites the tall giraffe.

That's why I'm sitting in my box...

just me.